HEAVENLY VISIONS

EYE WITNESSES OF PEOPLE WHO VISITED HEAVEN AND RETURNED.

D SUJAN

Made with ♥ on the Notion Press Platform
www.notionpress.com

HEAVENLY VISIONS

HEAVENLY ROMANYIC SYORIES.

These are two stories that a young girl by name Lydia DeCrosse dreamt.

She had visions of these stories from heaven...

SINCERE LOVE
- D. SUJAN

Natasha...! A beautiful girl as per the name, a suitable performance. Then I was studying first year of degree. I never felt like I could fall in love with a girl at first sight. Is it a charm? Or am I really in love? It took me a long time to learn that.

Christmas holidays were given in college. As always, I wanted to go to my grandmother's village and have fun. But, every day seemed like an era, don't look at Natasha. When will the holidays be over? When will I see Natasha? It seemed that.

On the first day of the college start, I went to the college before everyone else and looked for

Natasha. But, he did not come to college that day. She was afraid of what anyone would think if she asked.

Two days passed like that. As Natasha did not come to college anymore, today I went to her friend to find out the reason. Meanwhile, Natasha came. When I saw him, my face lit up like a 1000 volt light bulb.

Natasha is a very nice girl who doesn't talk too much with anyone. Studies well. I am an average student. As far as I know, he has never seen my face. When should I talk to him? When to be friends? When should I tell my love? While thinking.. A year has passed.

Even in the second year of the degree, I thought I should talk to him. It seems that God has given me a chance to talk to him, taking pity on my love. At the welcome party organized for the freshers, we both had to perform a play together. Seeing that as an opportunity, I got in touch with him and turned it into a friendship.

So... hiding my love for him in my heart and waiting to tell him when... the second year of my degree also passed. As always, she came as the class topper. I somehow passed out.

And the final year..., taking everyone's career very seriously, what to do next? Thinking that. Even if I close or open my eyes, I can see nothing but Natasha. The final year of the degree also comes to an end. Everyone is preparing well for the exams. There is nothing wrong with me because I did not listen to even one class properly.

Now I felt that if I don't tell my heart to Natasha, I will never be able to tell it again. I thought that I should somehow tell Natasha about my love in college the next day. I wrote about my love in a letter and sent it to him. The next day Natasha directly came to me. Is this your love or charm? I do not know. But, if you want to convince our people to marry me, at least you should pass your degree with good marks. So, she says let's see about this love marriage later, you should complete your degree first.

I took Natasha's words very seriously. I studied well and passed my degree in first class. Will you go to him and confess even now? I asked if it was my love. Then he thought that I told my parents about this love thing, but the degree is complete. What does Job do? How does he feed you? She asked. When I heard his words, I felt it was true.

Immediately I joined the Bachelor of Education. Luckily for me, I got a government teacher post notification after I completed my studies. I studied very hard and got a teacher's post. I can't believe myself. I passed my degree with passing marks, I passed in first class and now I have got a government job, it is because of Natasha.

My parents were very happy along with me. I can take responsibility for my two younger sisters. All of us at home are very happy that I can help my father in earning. The only delay is that I go to Natasha and tell her.

Natasha...! I got a good job as you said. They are also very happy in our house. I said that if you accept my love at this time, I will talk to you and convince you for our marriage. Waiting for his answer with heavy heart.

After a while of silence....! Look Aaron (she called me by name for the first time), listen to me carefully. Try to understand me. In our house, this love marriage is not accepted. I can't hurt my parents. There is a reason why I am telling you that.

That reason is my elder brother, he is the life of everyone in the house. While my parents were waiting for the grown up son to take over the responsibilities of the house and my marriage, he fell in love with a girl. She rejected that girl and my elder brother's love. She said crying that my elder brother had committed suicide without thinking about it with that fear and rage.

If, that day I told you that you don't want this love, I will leave you, what would you do? I thought that. As a good friend, I have come to advise you. I know that I am troubling you with my words and raising your hopes. I also know that you will be hurt when you know the truth. But life is more valuable than suffering...!

Now you got a good job. How happy are all your family members? You should be there for them. She said that you will surely find a girl suitable for your good heart and leave there.

Hearing all this, I wiped the water from my eyes and remained silent.
I thought about it all day. Till then Natasha was just a lover for me. But, from now on, she is a goddess for me. If he had really left me, I wouldn't be in such a good situation now. In fact, he would have survived the madness of love then?

Through his thoughts and words, I am what I am now. I also knew the responsibility. Natasha is the one who made me a better person, I replied to my mind.

After a few days.., my two younger sisters got married and I saw my father's smile in love. My mother saw a girl she liked and married me. He is my wife Svetlana who came into my life.

Svetlana knows everything about my past. I understand myself now we are happy with two children. My life is happy now because of two deities one is Natasha and the other is Svetlana.

PURE LOVE

- D. SUJAN

This love story is of Nick. Who didn't know anything about love. He was very happy with his life. He could do anything to make his friends happy. But he says that not all friends respect friendship.

All the friends of Lisa were her friends and for her money. But alas, Nick did not know anything about this. The days passed like this. One day that nature did a miracle. Lisa came to that college. And in the section in which Nick belonged.
All his friends went crazy after seeing Lisa. Lisa was very beautiful.

A friend of Nick fell in love with Lisa. He told all this to Nick. At this Nick laughed and said, "Hey man! What is this love? If you like her then go and tell Lisa directly. ,
On this the friend said, "What will happen if she does not agree?"
Nick said, "Don't be afraid, she will agree."

That friend did as his friend said. But Lisa did not agree. That friend became very sad. He told Nick about the Lisa's disobedience.

Nick explained to his friend and said, now I will bring Lisa for you.

Nick now started trying to bring the Lisa to himself. But Lisa did not trust any Nick so easily. It took him about three to four months just to talk. When the conversation started, everything started. Now everyday conversations started taking place, whether it was about home or outside.

Now both of them did every work together. Be it a college project or making notes.

Now Nick started spending more and more time with the Lisa. Nick spent least time with his friends. His friends didn't even like him.

One day his friend said to Nick, "You have brought Lisa for me. So you stay away from her."

Nick said, “Brother, she is yours.”

One day Nick thought why don’t I tell the whole story to Lisa. And give his love to my friend.

Thinking this Nick went to tell this thing to the Lisa. But as soon as he came in front of her, he felt afraid to say this.

Seeing the sadness on Nick’s face, the Lisa said, "What’s the matter, why are you sad?" If there is anything, tell me.

Nick said, “No no, it’s nothing.”

Then he went to his friends. But none of his friends saw his sadness. He began to understand how much his friends appreciated him. He did not say anything beyond this to any friend.

Then he went to his friends. But none of his friends saw his sadness. He began to understand how much his friends appreciated him. He did not say anything beyond this to any friend.

Now Nick slowly started falling in love with Lisa.

Now he started afraid of losing Lisa. When he thinks of Lisa, his friend comes to mind and when he thinks of his friend, Lisa comes to mind.

Meanwhile, Lisa's sister called Nick to meet her. His sister met Nick. He said, "If you guys ever need anything, I am with you." Both of you, don't betray anyone. ,

This thing shook Nick's soul. Now he was standing at a turn from where two roads were going. One towards friendship and the other towards love. He was not able to decide anything. But he says that you choose your own path. Otherwise time will choose your path. And you will be left with regrets.

Was in the last year of college. It's been

almost 6 months. His friends were now very angry with Nick. He wanted to take revenge from him.

It's just matter of one day. Nick was going home from his college. Then some of his friends came and he brought his friends with him. A friend of Nick said, "I told you to stay away from Lisa. But you will not believe it like this. You will understand everything when you get kicked.

Then that friend said to his friends, "Explain it well.,

Nick beat him a lot. And he went away from there.

Nick was so depressed that he did not even go to college for many days. Here Lisa used to wait for him every day. When he couldn't control the Lisa anymore, he asked her friends where she was.

None of her friends told anything about her. The Lisa became very upset. But what could she do now? After a few days Nick comes to college.

The Lisa asked Nick the reason for all this happening. Nick told him the whole thing. Whatever happened. He told that he had come to him for a friend.

Nick also told that he had asked his friend to give it to you. After hearing all this Lisa cried a lot.

The Lisa said, "I am not a toy that you can buy from a shop and give to your friend. I too have a heart and it has a heartbeat. If something like this had happened to me, tell me what you would have said and done."

After this the Lisa said, after today you should never show me your face. Come on, I made a mistake by trusting you."

Saying this Lisa left from there.

After this Nick tried very hard to talk to Nick.

But he could not succeed.

After a few days the college exams started. Both of them appeared for the exam. When the exam is over. So Lisa was never seen by Nick after this.

Nick searched for the Lisa a lot but could not find her anywhere. He also went to her house but his family members had gone away. Still Nick is still waiting for Lisa One day Nick gets a call from Lisa. His face brightens up.... To be continued..

My beloved is mine and I am his; he browses among the lilies. Until the day breaks and the shadows flee, turn, my beloved, and be like a gazelle or like a young stag on the rugged hills.

• How beautiful you are, my darling! Oh, how beautiful! Your eyes behind your veil are doves. Your hair is like a flock of goats descending from the hills of Gilead. Your teeth are like a flock of sheep just shorn, coming up from the washing. Each has its twin; not one of them is alone. Your lips are like a scarlet ribbon; your mouth is lovely. Your temples behind your veil are like the halves of a pomegranate. Your neck is like the tower of David, built with courses of stone; on it hang a thousand shields, all of them shields of warriors. Your breasts are like two fawns, like twin fawns of a gazelle that browse among the lilies. Until the day breaks and the shadows flee, I will go to the mountain of myrrh and to the hill of incense. You are altogether beautiful, my darling; there is no flaw in you.

• You have stolen my heart, my sister, my bride; you have stolen my heart with one glance of your eyes, with one jewel of your necklace. How delightful is your love, my sister, my bride! How much more pleasing is your love than wine, and the fragrance of your perfume more than any spice! Your lips drop sweetness as the honeycomb, my bride; milk and honey are under your tongue.

The fragrance of your garments is like the fragrance of Lebanon. You are a garden locked up, my sister, my bride; you are a spring enclosed, a sealed fountain. Your plants are an orchard of pomegranates with choice fruits, with henna and nard, nard and saffron, calamus and cinnamon, with every kind of incense tree, with myrrh and aloes and all the finest spices. You are a garden fountain, a well of flowing water streaming down from Lebanon. Awake, north wind, and come, south wind! Blow on my garden, that its fragrance may spread everywhere. Let my beloved come into his garden and taste its choice fruits. • I have come into my garden, my sister, my bride; I have gathered my myrrh with my spice. I have eaten my honeycomb and my honey; I have drunk my wine and my milk. Eat, friends, and drink; drink your fill of love.

• I slept but my heart was awake. Listen! My beloved is knocking: "Open to me, my sister, my darling, my dove, my flawless one. My head is drenched with dew, my hair with the dampness of the night." I have taken off my robe— must I put it on again? I have washed my feet— must I soil them again? My beloved thrust his hand through the latch-opening; my heart began to pound for him. I arose to open for my beloved, and my hands dripped with myrrh, my fingers with flowing myrrh, on the handles of the bolt.

I opened for my beloved, but my beloved had left; he was gone. My heart sank at his departure. I looked for him but did not find him. I called him but he did not answer. • My beloved is radiant and ruddy, outstanding among ten thousand. His head is purest gold; his hair is wavy and black as a raven. His eyes are like doves by the water streams, washed in milk, mounted like jewels. His cheeks are like beds of spice yielding perfume. His lips are like lilies dripping with myrrh. His arms are rods of gold set with topaz. His body is like polished ivory decorated with lapis lazuli. His legs are pillars of marble set on bases of pure gold. His appearance is like Lebanon, choice as its cedars. His mouth is sweetness itself; he is altogether lovely. This is my beloved, this is my friend, daughters of Jerusalem. • I am my beloved's, and my beloved is mine: he feedeth among the lilies.

• You are as beautiful as Tirzah, my darling, as lovely as Jerusalem, as majestic as troops with banners. Turn your eyes from me; they overwhelm me. Your hair is like a flock of goats descending from Gilead.Your teeth are like a flock of sheep coming up from the washing. Each has its twin, not one of them is missing.

Your temples behind your veil are like the halves of a pomegranate. Sixty queens there may be, and eighty concubines, and virgins beyond number; but my dove, my perfect one, is unique, the only daughter of her mother, the favorite of the one who bore her. The young women saw her and called her blessed; the queens and concubines praised her. • How beautiful your sandaled feet, O prince's daughter! Your graceful legs are like jewels, the work of an artist's hands.

NO GREATER LOVE THAN THIS THAT A MAN LAY DOWN HIS LIFE FOR HIS FRIEND.

JESUS LOVES YOU AND SAVES YOU. HE DIED AND PAID THE PRICE FOR YOUR SINS.
YOU WILL BECOME A NEW CREATION, NEW BODY, NEW MIND, NEW SOUL, IF YOU PRAY THIS"
JESUS, I ACCEPT YOU AS MY LORD AND SAVIOR IN MY HEART. FORGIVE ME AS YOU DIED FOR MY SINS. I FORGIVE MY ENEMIES .

ALL GLORY HONOUR PRAISE THANKS BE

TO GOD, JESUS HOLY SPIRIT. .

Contents

www.ingramcontent.com/pod-product-compliance
Lightning Source LLC
LaVergne TN
LVHW021203160826
845679LV00024B/2226